The
Missing Bird

by Sarah Moore
illustrated by Jiri Tibor Novak

SCHOOL PUBLISHERS

Requests for permission to make copies of any part of the work should be addressed to School Permissions and Copyrights, Harcourt, Inc., 6277 Sea Harbor Drive, Orlando, Florida 32887–6777. Fax: 407-345-2418.

HARCOURT and the Harcourt Logo are trademarks of Harcourt, Inc., registered in the United States of America and/or other jurisdictions.

Printed in the United States of America

ISBN 10: 0-15-351322-5
ISBN 13: 978-0-15-351322-0

Ordering Options
ISBN 10: 0-15-351211-3 (Grade 1 Advanced Collection)
ISBN 13: 978-0-15-351211-7 (Grade 1 Advanced Collection)
ISBN 10: 0-15-358034-8 (package of 5)
ISBN 13: 978-0-15-358034-5 (package of 5)

3 4 5 6 7 8 9 10   179   15 14 13 12 11 10 09 08

Characters: Jade
Kane
Ellen
Mr. Drake
Gus

Narrator: One day, Jade went to feed Gus, the class bird.

Jade: Oh, no! Gus is gone. He is not on his perch.

Kane: Gus is always in his cage.

Jade: Look, the cage door is open.

Narrator: The children are gathered near the cage.

3

Kane: How are we going to find him?

Jade: I know! Let's all chirp like a bird.

Ellen: Yes, when Gus hears us, he might come.

All: Chirp, chirp, chirp!

4

Mr. Drake: How come you are all chirping?

Jade: We're looking for Gus. He is missing from his cage.

Kane: All this chirping is making me tired.

Ellen: I could shake the bell in his cage.

Kane: Yes, when Gus hears the bell ring, he might come.

Narrator: Ellen shakes the bell, and they all look around for Gus.

Ellen: Gus might like some food to eat.

Jade: I have an apple in my bag.

Mr. Drake: That might get Gus to come back.

6

Narrator: Jade goes out and comes back with a big red apple.

Kane: I bet Gus would like to eat that—and so would I!

Mr. Drake: Let's put bits of apple by the cage for Gus.

Kane: He likes apples. He will come to eat, I think.

Narrator: Jade puts bits of apple by the cage. Just then, they see Gus fly out from the top of the bookshelf.

Ellen: Look! We have found Gus.

Narrator: Gus pecks at the yummy apple with his beak.

All: We're glad Gus likes apples so much!

8